W9-BFF-753

JOSH
A Boy with Dyslexia

Caroline Janover
Illustrated by Edward Epstein

WATERFRONT BOOKS
Burlington, Vermont 05401

For Michael

Copyright © 1988 by Waterfront Books and Caroline Janover

All rights reserved. No part of this book may be
reproduced in any form or by any means without
permission in writing from the publisher.

Fifth printing, October 1997

Distributed to the book trade by
Free Spirit Publishing Co.
400 First Avenue North
Suite 616
Minneapolis, MN 55401
1-800-735-7323

Designed and produced by Robinson Book Associates
Printed in the United States

Library of Congress Cataloging-in-Publication Data

Janover, Caroline.
   Josh : a boy with dyslexia.

   Summary: Josh struggles to live down the stigma of his learning
disability, dyslexia, and receive both respect and friendship from his
peers. Includes information on the characteristics of dyslexia and a
list of organizations that deal with learning disabilities.
   [1. Dyslexia–Fiction. 2. Learning disabilities–Fiction]
I. Epstein, Edward, 1936- ill. II. Title
PZ7.J2445Jo 1988   [Fic]   88-10661
ISBN 0-914515-10-7 paper
ISBN 0-914525-18-2 cloth

Chapter 1

On Sunday morning, Josh found a roach sleeping in his toothbrush. He turned the water on full blast and watched the bug swirl down the drain. He washed his toothbrush with soap and left it on the counter to dry.

"Time to get dressed." Josh's dad walked into his bedroom. He was carrying a gerbil cage on his hip. Gerbie and Herbie, the two gerbils, were huddled in the corner on top of a pile of sawdust. Dad stepped over a large, unpacked moving carton. He put the cage on top of Josh's desk.

"They've got to be in here somewhere," said Josh from the closet. His father ducked as a red slipper and a loafer flew toward him.

"Josh, this room is a wreck!" Dad picked up the loafer. "When are you going to get unpacked? It's a wonder you can find anything in this mess."

"Simon!" said Josh, narrowing his eyes. "Now I know where they are!" He marched past his father and into his brother's bedroom.

"Okay. Where are they?" he demanded.

"Where are who?" asked Simon, looking up from his crossword puzzle.

"Don't play dumb. What did you do with my sneakers?"

"You forgot to knock. Go back to the door and knock if you want to come into my room."

"Cut it out, Simon. Give me my sneakers!"

Simon smoothed out a wrinkle on his bedspread. His room was in perfect order. Every book was unpacked and arranged in the bookcase according to size and color. Simon used his swimming trophies as bookends.

"Stop yelling at me," said Simon calmly. "Besides, why would I want your sneakers anyway? I've got my own, see?" He wiggled his foot in front of Josh's face. Grabbing Simon's leg, Josh lunged at his older brother.

"Lay off," cried Simon, hitting the floor with a thud. "Now you'll *really* get it! Mom! Dad!" he shrieked, "Josh is teasing me. He attacked me for no reason!"

Mr. Grant appeared at the door. "All right, you guys, what's going on here?"

"My sneakers, Dad. Simon took them. He stole them and put them somewhere!"

"Prove it," replied Simon, straightening his socks.

"Why would Simon steal your sneakers? You probably just misplaced them, Josh."

"Yeah. You lose everything. Don't go blaming it on me!"

"I didn't! I didn't mis . . . mis . . lapse them!"

"The word is *misplace*, dummy," said Simon.

"Don't call me dummy!" Josh made a fist, ". . .or I'll pound you!" he threatened.

"That's enough!" said Mr. Grant sternly. "I thought

we'd get some peace and quiet now that you two have your own bedrooms." The boys looked at their feet.

"Simon, you come downstairs with me. I need help unpacking the book cartons." Mr. Grant turned to Josh. "And you, Josh. Don't be such a crybaby. Your shoes will turn up. Didn't I just tell you to get dressed? Now hurry up and brush your teeth, make your bed, and get some breakfast. And clean up that mess in your room!"

Josh stared out Simon's window. He watched a sparrow flittering around a tree and tried to remember where he'd last seen his red sneakers.

"Josh, are you listening to me?"

"Yes, Dad," he called after them. "What did you say? I forgot what you just said!"

Josh walked down the hall to the bathroom. He wiggled his toes in the new wall-to-wall grass green carpet. On the sink, he found his drying toothbrush. He smeared it with toothpaste and scrubbed his front teeth. Throwing his head back, he gargled with Simon's mouthwash.

"Can I come in?" His mother knocked twice on the bathroom door. "I need to get the clothes out of the hamper."

"Sure Mom," said Josh, spitting out the mouthwash. His mother had been painting. He liked the way she looked in her painting shirt. It was covered with splotches of paint. Paint stains, especially green, were under her fingernails and spattered all over her blue jeans.

"Mom, is today the first day of school?" Josh asked.

"No, lovey, it's tomorrow."

"How many days till tomorrow?"

"One day! Tomorrow is tomorrow." Mrs. Grant hugged her son and emptied the dirty clothes into a plastic laundry basket.

"I think I'll be sick on the first day of school," said Josh.

"Everyone is nervous the first day, Josh. I don't think you'll be sick. I think you'll do just fine."

"I don't think so."

"Why not?"

"I just ate germs."

"You ate germs?"

"Yeah. A roach laid germs on my toothbrush and I ate them. Now I can't go to school. I'll be too sick."

Mrs. Grant looked annoyed. "I don't believe it!" she cried. "The roaches must have gotten into the cartons when I packed up in the apartment. I'll call the exterminator this minute!" She grabbed the laundry basket and hurried out of the bathroom.

"Don't you even care that I'm about to get a disease?" Josh called after her. He sat down on the lid of the toilet seat. He wished P.J. had moved to New Jersey with them. P.J. had been his best friend since first grade. He didn't have a single friend in Ledgewood— not one.

Josh rested his head on his knees. He heard a dripping sound. He looked behind the toilet. Directly under the drip were his sneakers. They were sopping wet.

"I knew it," he said. "Simon's going to pay for this!" Josh picked up his brother's tube of pimple medicine from the sink. He made a pinprick with a safety pin through the middle of the tube. The flesh-colored cream began to ooze out of the hole. "That ought to do it!" he said with a smirk.

Josh sat back down on the toilet seat and tried to force his toes into the wet sneakers. He tied the damp

Mr. Grant took a big step and bumped into the wall.

laces. Whistling to himself, he stood at the top of the stairs. Simon and his father were still unpacking book cartons.

"Simon, give me a hand with this bookcase," said Mr. Grant, dusting the shelves. "It weighs a ton."

"Can I help?" called Josh, racing down the stairs. Mr. Grant picked up one end of the bookcase. Josh and Simon lifted the other.

"Which way?" asked his father, walking backward toward the living room.

"Go left," said Josh. Mr. Grant took a big step and bumped into the wall.

"I mean right!" said Josh quickly.

"You dip!" cried Simon. "Now look what you did. Mom just painted that wall and now it's all scratched up."

"Sorry," said Josh, "I got up mixed, I mean mixed up." He left Simon holding the bookcase and ran into the kitchen. Josh felt too upset to eat breakfast. Instead, he wrote his mother a note. He put the note on top of his cereal bowl and left it on the kitchen table.

I w9nt no mr dikɔ.

Lov

L. G.

Chapter 2

Josh rode his dirt bike full speed down Chestnut Street. At the end of the block he swerved into the road with the barking collie dog. Josh practiced popping wheelies. Flipping up on the front tire, he balanced for a few seconds on his rear tire. He pretended he was a stunt man about to jump burning buses.

"Think you're hot stuff, huh?" Josh looked over his shoulder, pressing down on the brakes. A fat kid with a baseball cap on backward pulled up next to him. He was riding a yellow ten-speed.

"You live around here?" He chomped on a wad of chewing gum.

"We just moved in," said Josh.

"Oh yeah? Where?" Josh looked up and down the block. He pointed behind him.

"I think it's down there."

"What grade are you going into?"

"Fifth." Josh bent down to retie his shoelace.

"I'm in seventh." He cracked his gum and offered Josh a piece. "Want one?"

"Thanks. I didn't eat breakfast."

"My name's Bucknell Biddleman III. You can call me Buck. What's yours?"

"Joshua Grant. We just moved here from New York City."

"You going to Valley School?" Josh stared at the ripples of fat under Buck's T-shirt. He nodded his head.

"Who's your teacher going to be?"

"I think her name is Mrs. Manertime."

"You mean Mrs. Mantimer?"

"Yeah, that's it."

"You're kidding! You're in Mantimer's class?" Buck chewed his gum faster.

"That's what my mom said."

"Are you some kind of mental? I mean, all of Man-

"My name's Bucknell Biddleman III. You can call me Buck."

timer's kids are weird. I mean, that's a special class, man."

Josh looked down at his damp red sneakers. He felt his feet begin to sweat. The blood pounded into his face. He could tell it was turning red.

"So?" said Josh, climbing back onto his bike seat. "I have a learning disability."

"You mean you're retarded?" asked Buck.

"I'm *not* retarded. I just have a mix-up in my brain. Sometimes I have trouble remembering things." Josh pushed off from the curb. "Thanks for the gum," he called as he pressed down hard on the pedals. His tanned legs had tight, strong muscles. He gripped the handlebars and sped down the street. Skidding around a corner, he turned into a street lined with tall, shady trees. Josh looked back—Buck had not followed him.

Josh got off his bike and rested at the curb. Standing on his tiptoes, he peered over prickle bushes into a yard. He saw a brick house with a birdbath in front. He'd never seen that house before. Josh felt the heat come around his face again. He ran his fingers through his curly brown hair. With his shirt sleeve, he wiped the sweat from his neck. He'd been lost before in Central Park. In New York you could ask people for directions. In New Jersey people didn't walk along the streets. They stayed inside their houses until it was time to come out and get inside their cars.

Josh squinted his eyes to read the street sign at the corner. It said Maple Street. He had memorized his new address, 138 Chestnut Street. The new phone number was 651-3586—or was it 651-3568? Josh scratched his head. Simon would know what to do. Josh looked for the wart on his thumb. That had to be his left hand because his left thumb had a wart.

"I'll go left," he said out loud. He pictured ice-cold orange juice waiting next to his bowl of Cheerios on the kitchen table. Josh heard a dog barking in the distance. It could be the collie dog one street away from his house. Josh pedaled in the direction of the bark. He knew he'd find his way home by lunchtime. He had to. Tomorrow was the first day of school. Besides, he was already beginning to feel sick.

Chapter 3

Mrs. Grant pulled up the shades to let in the morning light.

"Time to get up, Josh," she said softly. Josh did not move. Mrs. Grant sat down on the bed. She put her warm hand up under his shirt and gently rubbed his back.

"Time to get up, lovey."

"I'm too weak," he moaned, burying his head in the pillow.

"It's the first day of school, Josh."

"If I miss the first day, does that mean I have to be in the fourth grade all over again?"

"No, sweetheart. It just means you are absent the first day of the fifth grade."

"Then I'm too sick to go. I'm having a heart attack."

Mrs. Grant felt his forehead. "You don't have a fever."

"Of course, I don't have a fever. I have a heart attack." Josh pulled the covers up over his head.

"Come eat breakfast. You may feel better with food inside you." Josh sat up slowly. He pressed his right hand over his heart. He felt it pound under the alligator on his shirt. Josh always went to bed wearing his clothes. It saved time searching for an outfit in the morning.

Josh sat down next to his brother at the breakfast table. He smelled cologne and mint mouthwash. Simon's hair was wet and combed. Simon took showers without being asked. He was going into the seventh grade.

"This kid down the block named Buck says I've got the worst homeroom teacher in the school," Simon announced. "He says she has bad breath and she gives more homework than any of the other teachers."

Mrs. Grant looked up from the stove. She was making blueberry pancakes for the first day of school. "You're a good student, Simon," she said cheerfully. "I'm sure you can learn a great deal from Miss Potts. I've heard she has an excellent reputation."

Josh poked at the limp pancake on his plate. He'd never gotten a good report card in his life; not one single A. The teacher never put *his* papers up on the bulletin board. Last year, in the Resource Room, he hadn't even gotten one gold star on a spelling test.

"It's all Josh's fault we had to move here in the first place," grumbled Simon.

"My fault?"

"Yes, your fault. Just because you had to be in a special class for learning-disabled dummies."

"Simon!" Mrs. Grant glared at her son.

"You made us leave every friend we ever had and

"It's the first day of school, Josh."

our cozy apartment and the Adventure Playground in Central Park and—"

"Simon!" Mrs. Grant interrupted. "You know our apartment was too small. Besides, your father and I want you to grow up in the suburbs with more green space." She paused and flipped two pancakes.

"Ledgewood has an excellent school system."

Simon wiped blueberry stain off his teeth with his napkin. "Well, I'd be a lot happier if I were back in my old school and not in smelly Potts's class."

A ding-dong-ding rang through the house.

"What's that?" asked Josh.

"That's the back doorbell, you dip!" Simon shoved back his chair and hurried to the door. "Hi Buck," he said happily. "Mom, this is Buck Biddleman, the kid I was telling you about. Buck, this is my mom."

Mrs. Grant wiped her hands with a dish towel. "Nice to meet you, Buck," she said shaking his hand. "What grade are you going into?"

"I'm in Mr. Manfrini's seventh grade." Buck chomped on his gum and stared at Josh.

"Are you boys all going to walk to school together?" Mom asked.

"Nope." Simon slung his bookbag over his shoulder. "Buck and I are going to ride our bikes. I promised him we'd ride together on the first day."

"Oh!" Mrs. Grant looked uneasy. "Well, have a good day, boys. I'll see you at lunchtime."

Josh heard the screen door slam.

"It's my heart," he moaned as he slumped down over his plate, careful not to get syrup in his hair. "I'm too weak to make it to school." Josh could see his mother was upset. She wet her lips with her tongue and stared out the kitchen window.

"Okay, Josh, just for today and today only, I'll drive you to school. After today, you ride your bike."

Josh felt relief. He wasn't sure he could find Valley Elementary School, at least not without Simon to show him which way to go.

"Besides," his mother said, "it's only a half day today. I'm sure you have the strength to make it through the morning."

Josh put his arms around his mother's waist. He leaned his head against her soft tummy. "Okay Mom, I'll go," he said, "but only if you drive me *and* pick me up at lunchtime."

His mother nodded. In the car she put on her dark glasses and took a Kleenex out of her purse. She blew her nose. Josh thought that was odd. It was a cloudy day and his mother didn't have a cold.

Chapter 4

Josh hoped he'd have a desk in the last row. He didn't want to sit next to a girl. He wanted a window on one side and a boy on the other.

"Come right in," Mrs. Mantimer said, smiling. "You must be our new student from New York City." She walked toward Josh to shake hands. He glanced at the wart on his thumb. That reminded him not to shake with the left hand. He held out his right hand and looked Mrs. Mantimer in the eye.

"Hello," he said. "My name is Joshua Grant."

"We're so happy to have you, Joshua. Would you like to choose your desk? You can tape this name card to whatever desk you'd like." She handed Josh a strip of construction paper with his name neatly printed in black ink.

Josh was surprised to see only ten desks in the classroom. He chose one in the last row next to the window. Sunlight filled the large cheerful room and plants hung in baskets from the ceiling next to the teacher's desk.

Mrs. Mantimer stood in front of the class. She had curly grey hair. The teacher began to introduce each child to the class. There were seven boys and three girls. Josh looked carefully to see if he fit in. Everyone looked pretty cool. Three of the boys wore alligator shirts like his. One boy had a T-shirt with words written on it. Josh read: *My Mow anb Dab went to Floriba and all I got saw this bump T-shrit.*

Mrs. Mantimer smiled at Josh. "Perhaps you'd like to tell the boys and girls where you lived in the city," she said.

"Huh?" asked Josh nervously.

"What street did you live on in New York?"

"Oh, Eighty-fourth Street. Near the park."

"Is that Central Park?"

"Yeah. I mean yes. Yes, it is. Near Central Park, I mean."

Mrs. Mantimer wrote the words *New York City* and *Central Park* on the blackboard. "Let's say these words, together," she said, pointing to each. As the class repeated the words, Josh leaned over to the boy sitting next to him.

"Do you need permission to go to the bathroom?" he whispered.

"Just tell Mantimer. She's decent. She'll let you go any time." Josh read the name taped to the boy's desk. It was *Davib.*

Mrs. Mantimer sat on a tall stool in front of the class. "Just to review and ease back into the school spirit, who'd like to come to the board and mark the words with one syllable? Lauren, how about you?" Lauren went forward and selected a piece of pink chalk. She began to circle words.

"Do you need permission to go to the bathroom?" Josh whispered.

"You like the teacher?" Josh asked David.

"Oh yeah! She never yells. My mom says she has the patience of a saint."

"Lauren, that's very good!" said Mrs. Mantimer. "You have a splendid memory. Now, who will mark the words with two syllables? How about it, Todd?" Lauren sat down and Todd took her place at the blackboard.

"Do you get much homework?" whispered Josh.

"Not really. Each kid gets different homework 'cuz we work at our own speed."

Josh remembered back to last year in New York City. His teacher used to pound his reading book. Once she screamed at him in front of the whole class. She said he was too slow and messy to be in her reading group. She said he was lazy and he never paid attention. When she said that, Josh went into the bathroom and threw up.

Josh blinked and looked back at the blackboard. "Terrific, Todd!" said Mrs. Mantimer. "That's absolutely correct. I can see we're off to a great start. I have the feeling we're going to have a *very* good year!"

Chapter 5

The dismissal bell rang at noon. Josh put his homework in his bookbag. David led the line to the front door. They walked down the long, dark hall and out into the sunlight. "How come all schools smell the same? My school in New York smelled exactly like this one."

"Floor wax," said David.

"Floor wax? What do you mean, floor wax?"

"My uncle sells school supplies. He says most schools buy the same floor wax." Josh nodded in agreement.

"Do you live near Chestnut Street?" he asked David.

"No, I live on the other side of town, close to the movie theater." Josh wanted to invite him over for lunch. Before he could say anything, David darted toward another friend. "See you tomorrow," he yelled, disappearing behind a parked car.

Josh stood alone. He looked through the mob of children for his mother's car. She had a parking space directly in front of the school. She must have come early to watch for him. When Josh climbed into the front seat, his mother gave him a hug.

"How was it?" she asked.

"Okay," said Josh with a grin. "I like my teacher. She has the patience of a saint." He put his foot up on the seat and tied his shoelaces.

"What about the other kids?" his mother asked.

"They're nice, too. I made one friend. I forget his name. I sit right next to him. He showed me how to sign out for the bathroom."

Josh saw his mother pull in her breath and let out a sigh of relief.

"I hate the first day of school," she said, starting the car. "It makes me so nervous."

"It makes *you* nervous? Think of me! I'm starving. Can we go to Burger King for lunch?"

"Not today, lovey. I've got to get back to work. Besides, I want to be home when Simon gets back."

"Mom, the nurse says for you to look for head lights."

"What for?"

"She says head lights are catching. She said that in health class."

"Oh, you mean head *lice!*" His mother smiled. "Don't worry. I'll check your head every Sunday night when you wash your hair."

Josh liked the crunching sound of the gravel when the car drove up the steep driveway. He saw Simon's ten-speed bike leaning against the garage door. Simon was making two peanut butter and jelly sandwiches when they walked into the kitchen.

"How was school, Simon?" asked Mrs. Grant as she

put her purse next to the toaster. Simon didn't look up. "It was terrible," he groaned. "Miss Potts is a real hag. Her breath smells exactly like Dad's lawn fertilizer. You should see the homework she gives, even on the first day!"

Mrs. Grant smiled and poured two glasses of milk. "You'll live, Simon," she said. "I'll stay while you eat lunch. After that, I've got to get back to the bank. I get ten minutes more for lunch here than I did in the city."

"I'm going out after lunch," said Simon. "A bunch of us are going to play kickball in the park."

"Can I come?" asked Josh.

"No way!"

"Why not?"

"Because you always pull a hyper when you're not winning. That's why."

"I promise I won't lose my temper."

"You're such a baby. In baseball you quit just because you can't hit the ball."

"I'll be a good sport. I promise. I won't quit. I'll be perfect."

Mrs. Grant put the peanut butter back on the shelf. Simon rinsed his plate and put it in the dishwasher. "What time will you be home, Mom?" he asked.

"I'll be back by five. Keep an eye on your brother. You know the number at the bank if there's an emergency." Mrs. Grant put her purse strap over her shoulder. She kissed the boys good-bye. Josh watched to see if Simon's kiss was longer. Then he heard the car motor start. He listened for the crunch of gravel as his mother backed the car down the drive.

"Please, Simon, let me come with you!"

"Okay, if you promise not to act like a wimp."

"I promise," said Josh. He put his dishes in the dishwasher. Then he tied his sneakers again. Simon knew how to make double knots. His sneakers never came untied.

Eight kids were already playing kickball when Josh and Simon rode up to Citizen's Park. Buck said he wanted Simon on his team. Josh didn't know anyone on the other team. He joined it without complaining.

"No grenading," yelled a tall kid in the sixth grade. He had eyeglasses and ears that stood out like white mushrooms. Josh wondered what grenading meant. He didn't dare ask. They might know he'd never played kickball before.

Josh watched as Buck kicked a high fly into the lilac bush. "Interference!" cried the tall kid. Buck kicked again. The ball whizzed past Josh and into outer field. A girl behind him caught the ball. She tagged Buck out at third base.

"Nice going, Betsy," said a kid who looked like he was in first or second grade. Simon was up next. Josh thought he looked tough, standing there chewing gum and spitting onto the lawn. Simon kicked a foul into the street. The ball rolled down the block. A girl with stringy, wet hair chased after it. She heaved the ball back into center field. Simon kicked again. The ball shot past third base and into left field. Simon ran the

−23−

bases and slid into home plate.

"Man, you can run!" cried Buck. He slapped his buddy on the back. "Nice going, man." Simon blew a bubble the size of a grapefruit. "What's the score?" he asked, even though he knew his team was winning. The next guy up struck out. The players in the field trotted toward home plate.

Josh was up after a girl in designer jeans. She was safe at first base. The pitcher rolled Josh a spinner. He kicked the ball with all his power. His foot sprang into midair and flopped back down. "Strike!" yelled the pitcher. Keeping his eye focused on the ball, Josh gave another powerful kick. This time the ball rocketed into center field. Josh ran. He raced his

"You're going the wrong way!" screamed voices from all over the field.

fastest. "You're going the wrong way!" screamed voices from all over the field. Josh slid into base—third base!

"You dip, you ran the wrong way!" he heard Buck say. Josh froze. Buck was in midfield laughing like crazy. "That kid's an idiot," he yelled. "He's one of Mantimer's mentals." Other kids pointed and laughed.

"Knock it off," shouted Simon. "So he went the wrong way! Big deal! Let's get on with the game. We'll call it a foul."

Josh looked at Simon gratefully and walked back to home plate. He kicked again. He missed the ball. "Strike out," called the pitcher. Josh walked over to the curb and sat down. He put his head between his legs. He wanted to ride his bike home and lock himself in the bathroom. He wished he hadn't promised Simon he wouldn't quit.

"Don't feel too bad," said a voice beside him. Josh looked up. The girl with the wet, stringy hair sat down beside him. "Sometimes kids just get nervous and go the wrong way. It's happened before. Once Bruce McFay did that." The girl chewed on a strand of wet hair. "What's your name?" she asked.

"Josh. We just came here from New York City. We don't play kickball in New York. I think it's a stupid game."

"I love kickball," said the girl.

"Then how come you aren't playing?" asked Josh.

"My mom won't let me."

"Why not?"

"'Cause I got lice. She just washed my hair with special shampoo. That's why it's wet."

Josh wanted to move farther down the curb. He decided that wouldn't be polite.

"When my hair dries, my mom has to look for lice eggs. When all the nits are out, I can go back to school."

"You mean you can't go to school?"

"Nope. I can't even play kickball."

"What's your name?"

"Kelly. That's my brother, Buck, over there." She pointed to the pitcher. Josh stood up and stretched. He bent down and retied his shoe lace. "I've got to get back to the game," he said.

"Good luck," said Kelly, tossing her long hair over her shoulder. "I'll see you around."

Josh walked back to the game. He wondered how long kickball games lasted. He wanted to lie down and rest his heart. He wanted to curl up in the pillows on the couch and watch cartoons. Instead, he stayed at Citizen's Park. He stayed even after he heard the first distant roll of thunder. Standing on third base, he felt a drop of rain. It landed on his arm. Josh looked at his bike propped against a tree.

"I've got to get my bike in the garage before it melts—I mean rusts!" he called to the tall kid. He ran from third base toward the tree. Swinging himself onto the bike, he began to quickly pedal home. Josh didn't look back. He didn't care if Buck called him a scaredy cat. He wanted to get inside his house before the lightning came closer. Once Josh had been so scared in a thunderstorm, he'd wet his pants.

Chapter 6

The next morning, on the way to school, Josh found an anthill between the cracks on the sidewalk. He got off his bike and sat down on the ground to examine the tiny black insects. Ants must have lots of friends, he thought. They always seem to be together. Josh picked out the biggest leader ant. He pretended that was him.

He was startled by a voice.

"What are you doing?" Kelly stopped and knelt down beside him.

"Oh, nothing, just looking at some ants."

"You'll be late for school. I'm late myself. My mom had to look for more lice eggs. If the nurse can't find any, I can go back to class."

"You mean you got rid of your lice?" Josh asked.

"I hope so."

"Do lice walk around on your clothes?"

"Nope, lice can't live long out of your head. They need the warmth of your body. My cousin read a book about a king who died. It was in the olden days. When he died and got cold, all the lice ran off him into the bed sheets."

"That's gross," said Josh. He stood up and began to wheel his bike toward the Valley Elementary School.

"How'd you like that thunderstorm last night?" asked Kelly. "Wasn't it great when the electricity went out?"

"I hate thunderstorms," said Josh. He swallowed, hoping his throat might be too sore to go to school.

"What's the worst thunderstorm you were ever in?" Kelly asked.

"Once me and my mom and dad and Simon went to Ike's farm down in the South."

"Who's Ike?"

"What are you doing," asked Kelly.
"Oh, nothing. Just looking at some ants."

"I don't know. I think he's an uncle or a niece of my mom's."

Kelly looked confused. "Go on," she said.

"A thunderstorm came over the mountains. It got so close that lightning came out of the plugs in the living room. Lightning hit a tree in the field. When the storm ended, we went down to look, and Ike blew a hyper. He almost went crazy. Six of his cows got dead because they stood under the tree. They got zapped alive."

Kelly chewed on the end of her pigtail. "Buck once told me that a boy was electrocuted because he was peeing on a tree when it was hit by lightning."

"No kidding?" said Josh in amazement. He reminded himself never to go to the bathroom in a thunderstorm, even in the toilet.

"Out of the way!"

Josh turned around. Simon and Buck were pedaling down the street toward them at top speed. He hopped on his bike.

"Hi, guys," he called. "Wait up."

"It's one of Mantimer's mentals," cried Buck as he whizzed past.

"Shut up, Wrinkle Belly!" yelled Josh. "You look funny, but looks aren't everything!"

Kelly giggled. "Your brother is a real creep," Josh said. "What did I ever do to him?"

"He's just that way," said Kelly. "He picks on kids, especially kids younger. It drives my parents crazy."

When Josh got to class, Mrs. Mantimer was already

taking attendance. She had put three papers on his desk. He read over his daily schedule. First he had to correct the three papers. Then at 9:00 it said to go to art class with 5G. Josh raised his hand. "Who is 5G?" he asked.

"You're going to go to art, gym, and music with Mrs. Ginsberg's fifth grade class, Josh. There are some great kids in that class. You'll like them."

Grown-ups didn't understand about making friends. Josh sneezed. Maybe he was getting a cold. He imagined the school nurse calling his mother in her office at the bank. "Take your son home immediately," she'd say. "His throat is flaming red." The nurse would advise bed rest and plenty of fluids. He'd be allowed to drink coke and watch TV all day. If Mrs. Mantimer sent home school work, he'd say his eyes were too tired to focus on words.

At nine o'clock there was a knock on the door. A boy with mussed-up hair and freckles came in.

"Hello Kip," said Mrs. Mantimer. "You certainly did grow over the summer!"

"That's what everyone says." He grinned. "I've come to pick up Joshua Grant. Mrs. Ginsberg says he's supposed to come to art with us."

Josh stood up at his desk. "Do I need my pencil?" he asked.

"No, just your smock," said Kip. "They've got lots of stuff to draw with in the art room."

Josh put on his father's old cotton shirt and rolled

up the long sleeves. It had blue ink stains on the pocket.

"Do you miss your old school?" asked Kip as they walked down the hall.

"Not really. But I miss my friends, especially P.J. He was my best friend since first grade."

"I hear they've got a lot of muggers in New York City and dirty movies."

"Nah, I never saw any dirty movies. That's an agerexation. I mean exaggeration."

"Ledgewood's a pretty good town," said Kip. "We've got a town pool and lots of sports teams. You like art?" he asked, buttoning his smock.

"Art's okay, but I like gym better. I've always been a pretty decent runner."

"We get to go to gym tomorrow," said Kip opening the door to the art rooom. "Sit next to me," he whispered, pointing to a large table.

The art room was bright. It had large picture windows with red geranium plants arranged along the sills. There were pictures by famous artists hanging on the walls. Mr. Moody leaned against a huge sink.

"Welcome, boys and girls," he said, as he adjusted the red handkerchief in the pocket of his brown corduroy jacket. He wore a turtleneck instead of a shirt and tie, and he had a blue and white striped kitchen apron tied around his waist.

"I'd like to welcome you all to another year in the art room. I'd especially like to welcome Joshua Grant from Mrs. Mantimer's class and the five new boys and girls from Mrs. Ginsberg's room. I'll do my best to remember your names but, at my age, the memory isn't what it used to be." He took off his glasses and rubbed his eyes. Josh thought he looked tired, even on the second day of school.

"What do you bet he'll make us draw a picture of something we did over the summer," whispered a girl with pigtails.

Mr. Moody passed around art paper, Magic Markers, and colored pencils. "Children, I'd like you to think back to last summer." He cleared his throat. "Think of a moment you'll never forget. Perhaps it was a moment of wondrous surprise or horrifying terror. Perhaps you'd like to draw your family on a special trip or outing. I'll give you twenty minutes to draw and then I'll ask for a few volunteers to share their Summer Memory pictures with the class. Are there any questions?"

"Do we have to fill up the whole paper?"

"That is up to you, my friend." Mr. Moody began to wander around the room, chatting with the students.

"I knew it," said the girl with the pigtails. "I'm going to draw the same Summer Memory picture I've made since second grade. It's like a tradition. I always draw me on the beach with my dog Waggs, only Waggs died."

"How did he die?" asked the girl next to her.

"It was terrible. We were up in Maine and he got

attacked by a porcupine. Quills were all over him, especially on his nose. He was thirteen years old and he couldn't stand the pain. The vet put him to sleep.

Josh pictured important events in his summer. He remembered when the moving men let him carry Gerbie and Herbie's cage into the gigantic moving truck. The worst moment was when he had to say goodbye to P.J. They were at a playground in Central Park. P.J. picked a scab off a mosquito bite so they could be blood brothers forever. A best moment was going fishing with his grandfather on Cape Cod. Josh drew blue waves with white caps on them. He took a charcoal pencil from the basket in the center of the table and began to sketch a boat.

"You're a good artist," said Kip. "How come you're in Mantimer's class?"

"I've got dyslexia."

"What's that, some kind of disease?"

"No way," said Josh, drawing in his grandfather holding a fishing rod. "It just means I have trouble reading and remembering things. I've got great ideas but sometimes I can't spell too good when I write things down."

"Can you catch dyslexia?"

"You're born with it. Millions of people have it, even famous people."

"Yeah, like who?"

"Like Thomas Edison who made the first light bulbs, and Bruce Jenner."

"You mean the guy on cereal boxes? He's cool, man.

We have a VCR and my dad rented a movie of the Olympics and I saw him win the decathlon."

"Oh, yeah, I know," said Josh proudly. "He's even in TV commercials."

"You want to race me after school? We could meet at the bike rack at 3:05. I bet you're a great athlete, like Bruce Jenner."

"Sure, I'll race you," said Josh. "Back in New York I was the fastest in my class."

Josh sketched a fish at the end of his grandfather's fishing line. He could tell that the girl with pigtails had been watching him. Then, he heard her whisper to her friend, "I think Josh is cute!"

Chapter 7

Josh took out his homework notebook and copied down the math assignment. He liked the way Mrs. Mantimer wrote all the assignments on the blackboard. He hadn't forgotten to do his homework once; not like last year. Sometimes in New York, he'd taken the wrong book home or done the wrong assignment.

Josh zipped up his bookbag and threw it over his shoulder. When the dismissal bell rang Mrs. Mantimer asked him to lead the line to the front exit. Josh held the heavy main door open as streams of students poured out into the warm afternoon sunshine.

In the crowd of kids hanging around the bike rack, Josh saw Kelly. She was talking to the girl with the pigtails.

"Ready to race?" called Kip, running toward him. "I almost had to stay after," he panted, "but I told Mrs. Ginsberg I had a dentist appointment so she let me out."

"Good thinking! Where shall we run to?"

"Let's run to that telephone pole and back," said Kip.

"Okay. Maybe Kelly could hold out her arms and be the finish line," Josh suggested.

Kip and Josh ran towards Kelly's outstretched arms.

"Hey, Kelly, come over here." Kip called. "Want to be a finish line?"

"Sure, I'll be your finish line," she said.

Josh flung his bookbag aside. He knelt and took a starting position, with Kip right beside him.

"On your mark—get set—go!" shouted Kelly.

The boys raced to the telephone pole. Kids stopped to watch, cheering as Kip and Josh touched the pole at the same moment, turned around, and ran toward Kelly's outstretched arms.

"Josh by a hair!" yelled Kelly. "I felt his hand first!"

"Nice going," cried Simon, patting his brother on the back.

"You can really run!" said Kelly's friend, twisting her pigtail. "I think you're faster than my brother and he's in seventh grade."

"Gee, thanks," said Josh, grinning.

"So you beat one of Mantimer's mentals? What's so great about that, Kip?" Josh looked up and saw Buck sitting on his yellow ten-speed.

"He beat *me*," Kip replied. "And so what if he's in Mantimer's class? He's a fast runner and he's my friend."

Buck folded his arms. "Anyone can see he's a retard."

"Knock it off, Buck," cried Simon. "Leave the kid alone."

"Okay," said Buck as he blew an enormous pink bubble. "I'll leave him alone. Who wants to play with mentals anyhow?"

"I wouldn't talk, Wrinkle Belly," said Josh.

"Don't call me Wrinkle Belly," Buck warned.

"Well, then don't call me a mental!"

"I'll call you anything I please," yelled Buck.

Josh pushed Kip and Simon out of his way. He marched up to Buck, made a fist, and punched him in the stomach. Buck lost his balance and fell off his bike. He landed in a pile of soggy, wet leaves. Josh jumped on his back and began pounding him with his fists.

"Break it up!" said Simon, pulling at his brother's shirt. "What, are you crazy, Josh? You want to get us all in trouble? What if the principal sees us?"

Buck stood up and peeled a glob of pink bubble gum

off his cheek. "That didn't even hurt," he said, getting back on his bike.

"Come on, Simon, let's go fishing." Pedaling away, he called back, "and remember, we don't fish with mentals!"

Josh watched as Buck and Simon rode together out of the schoolyard. He grabbed his bike and pushed his way through the crowd.

"So long, Josh," called Kip.

Josh didn't look back. He didn't even say good-bye.

When Josh got home, he took the house key from

Buck landed in a pile of soggy, wet leaves.

the secret hiding place behind the porch thermometer. He let himself into the empty house. It was silent inside and smelled of Lemon Pledge. Josh walked into the kitchen and took a peach yogurt out of the refrigerator. Then he flipped on the TV and slumped into his dad's leather chair. As a football rerun came flickering onto the screen, Josh imagined himself as the star quarterback. He'd be playing in the Super Bowl. A huge hulk from the opposing team comes barging straight toward him. Bam! Josh knocks him flat. Through all the blood, Josh recognizes his old enemy, Buck. "Sorry, Fang Face," he says. "I guess I just knocked out your front tooth." It takes four guys to carry Buck off the field on a stretcher. The crowd goes wild.

A dog food commercial snapped Josh out of his daydream. He decided to ride his bike over to the place where the ants lived. He propped his bike against a chestnut tree and began to look for the big leader ant.

"Hi, Josh," said Kelly, walking toward him pushing a baby carriage. Josh dropped a chestnut through the metal grate over the storm drain. Kelly sat down on the curb beside him. "This is Willy. I babysit for him every Wednesday."

"Your brother is the world's biggest creep."

"You're telling me!" said Kelly. "What did he do now?"

"He called me a mental! Did you see that? Right in front of everybody he called me a mental! I hate that guy."

Kelly waved a chestnut in front of the baby. "It could be worse," she said.

"What do you mean?"

"He could be *your* brother!"

"Thanks a lot. Simon's bad enough."

"Maybe Buck said that because you're in Mantimer's class." Kelly looked at the ground. She shuffled her feet in the yellow leaves.

"It's not my fault I have a learning disability. I was born that way. It makes me pissed. How come my brain got messed up and not Simon's? It just isn't fair!"

"No, it isn't," said Kelly. "But you're a fast runner. Last year Kip was the fastest kid in the fourth grade."

"No kidding!" Josh dropped another chestnut into the drain.

"I know what I can do!" he said. "I'll ambush Buck and Simon when they get back from fishing." Josh jumped up and tied his shoe. Kelly and the baby watched while he collected handfuls of chestnuts.

"It'll be great! They won't even know what hit them!" Humming to himself, Josh began to fill his bike basket with chestnuts.

Chapter 8

Josh lay on his bed pretending to read. He looked at the pictures and thought about the ambush. It was wonderful! He'd hit Simon on the ear with a chestnut. Josh sat up when he heard his father's footsteps coming up the stairs.

"Josh, if you're ready to apologize to Simon, you may come downstairs and have dinner with us." Josh stared at his book.

"Well? I'm losing patience with you, Joshua."

"It wasn't my fault, Dad. He should apologize to me."

"For what? You can't just go around attacking people for not inviting you to go fishing."

"Is that what he said?"

"Is there more to the story?"

"Never mind," said Josh, avoiding his father's eyes.

"If you want to be stubborn and stay in your room, it's all right with me, but your mother would like you to join us."

"Okay. I'm coming," said Josh, sliding off the bed.

Josh walked into the kitchen.

"Anyone seen more roaches?" he asked.

"Thank heavens, no—not since the exterminator

came," said Mrs. Grant, wiping the counter with a sponge.

"I wonder if we could use roaches for bait," said Simon. "That would save me digging up all those worms in mom's vegetable garden."

Josh set the table while Simon poured the milk. The family sat down to dinner. Mrs. Grant passed a platter of corn on the cob.

"You dip! When will you ever learn the fork goes on the left? The *knife* goes on the right." Simon rearranged his silverware.

"Take it easy," said Mrs. Grant. "It's not the end of the world."

"How come Josh always gets special treatment? If he's going to set the table he should—"

"Didn't you hear what your mother said?" Mr. Grant interrupted. "Take it easy."

"So how was your day, Simon?" asked Mr. Grant.

"Okay. I got a ninety-seven on my first spelling test."

"Great! And what about you Josh? What did you do in school today?"

"Nothing."

"What did you do after school?"

"Played."

"I caught a sunny at Gypsy Pond," said Simon. "There were lots of kids from school there. We're thinking of starting a fishing club."

Josh looked at Simon and then down at his plate. Leaning his head on his hand, he began to poke holes in his pork chop.

"Buck and I are going to be the officers." Simon went on. "Maybe I'll be president and Buck will be vice-president."

Mr. Grant took a sip of his drink and turned to Josh. "Don't *slouch* at the table, Josh. And stop playing with your food."

Josh took his knife and carefully pushed the gravy off his pork chop.

"There are no cucumbers or lima beans in that gravy, Josh," said Dad, getting angry. "Sit up and eat like a man!"

"Here, let me cut that for you, lovey." Mrs. Grant leaned over and began to cut Josh's meat.

"Susan, don't baby him. Let him do it himself."

"I'm not babying him, Ben."

"If you weren't always trying to do everything for him, maybe he'd finally learn to do something right for himself."

"Don't slouch at the table, Josh."

Josh grabbed the knife from his mother and began sawing wildly at the pork chop. Then he jumped up from the table, ran upstairs, and slammed the bedroom door.

Josh yanked open the top drawer of his dresser. He took out clean underwear for the next morning. He undressed and threw his dirty clothes under the bed. Stepping out of his untied sneakers, he pulled on his clean pants and shirt and buckled his belt. He climbed under the covers and pulled the sheet over his head. Josh tried to think about his multiplication facts. Instead, he kept thinking about the fishing club. Buck and Simon would never let him join. He'd come home from school and the street would be deserted. Every kid on the block would be in the club, even girls. Josh put his head under the pillow and tried to go to sleep.

Chapter 9

Josh looked out the classroom window. He saw a robin pecking for worms. Worms reminded him of bait. Bait reminded him of the fishing club. He swung his feet back and forth fast underneath the desk.

"Josh, time for your reading group," said Mrs. Mantimer. Josh stood up and walked to the reading table at the back of the room. He saw David practicing his cursive writing at the blackboard. He wished David were in his reading group.

"Now that we've decided which children will read together, we need to choose a name for each group. Any suggestions?"

Josh had an idea but he didn't dare say it out loud. He wanted to call the group "The Duds." Back in New York he was always in the worst reading group. He constantly lost his place. By the time he sounded out each word, he'd forget what the sentence said.

"Last year we had "The Sharks," "The Beetles," and "The Cosmos," said Mrs. Mantimer, passing out the books. "What will it be this year?"

"How about "The Astros?" said a boy, making teeth marks in his pencil.

"Yeah! That's a good idea," said another kid.

"What do you think, Josh?" asked Mrs. Mantimer.

"It's okay with me." Josh looked at the reading book. He hoped he wouldn't have to read out loud.

"Great," said Mrs. Mantimer. "Before we begin, I'll give you each a bookmark. I know how hard it is to keep your place, especially when you're reading out loud."

Mrs. Mantimer smiled at Josh. She pointed to the title of the story. "Why don't you start us off?"

Josh took a deep breath. "Ab-ven-tr in oo-tr psake, I mean space."

"So what is the title of our story?"

"Adventure in Outer Space." He could tell that by looking at the picture of a man in a white space suit.

"That's exactly right, Josh. First we'll discuss new vocabulary words. Then I'll ask you each to read the first paragraph silently. After that, perhaps we'll have a volunteer read the paragraph out loud." Josh took another deep breath. Being an "Astro" was better than being a dud in New York City.

After reading, Mrs. Mantimer flicked the light switch on and off. Everyone stopped talking and froze like statues.

"You children have worked so well this morning, I think it's time for a break. How about a game of Simon Says?" David stood in front of the class. Each student stood next to his desk except Josh. He sat in his chair. He folded his arms over his chest and frowned.

David began, "Simon says put your left hand over your right ear and then stamp your right foot."

The kids giggled. "Okay, Lauren, you're out," said David. "You stamped your left foot!"

While the game continued, Mrs. Mantimer walked over to Josh's desk. "Come on, Josh. You try, too."

"I don't want to play."

"Everyone plays. It's fun. It doesn't matter if you don't do it perfectly."

"I thought we were supposed to learn to read in here, not play stupid baby games. Can I go to the nurse's office?"

"Don't you feel well?"

"If I can't go to the nurse's office, can I go to the bathroom? Please?"

"I think you should try to play the game, Josh."

"I won't play! You can't make me!"

"Josh, step into the hall with me for a second." Josh followed Mrs. Mantimer into the corridor.

"Is something wrong, Josh? I've never seen you act like this before."

"Yeah, something is wrong!" Josh blurted out. "How come people named Simon always get to give the orders? They think they rule the world."

"It's just a game, Josh. Would it be better if we called it Sam Says or Herman Says?"

"Yeah. That would be better—much better."

"Does your brother give you a hard time?"

"Yeah. He teases me. He's been teasing me every day since I got born." Josh ran his fingers through his hair. "Simon's so lucky. He always finishes his homework before I do. He gets to watch extra TV. He's in the gifted and talented program and he gets to watch 'Crime Story.'"

"But you work hard, too, Josh."

"I work hard but things just fall out of my brain. My mom says I'm not stupid but I think it's the ostipit, I mean opposite."

"Josh, you can learn anything in this world you want to learn. It may take extra time, drill, and practice, but you'll get it. You are not stupid, by any means."

"Oh yeah? How can you tell?"

"Because you have a high I.Q. Not only that, I've watched how hard you work. As a matter of fact, I was going to call your parents this weekend to say what a fine job you are doing in my class."

"You were? Will you talk to my dad?"

"Absolutely. I'd be delighted to talk to your dad."

Josh followed Mrs. Mantimer back into the classroom. He stood next to his desk and felt for the wart on his left thumb.

"Simon says for Josh to hop on his right foot to the blackboard," said Lauren. Josh hopped to the front of the classroom. Lauren sat down. Josh grinned and said, "Herman says spin three times and fall under your desk!"

Chapter 10

Josh woke up with an itch on top of his head. He prayed it was lice so he'd have to stay home from school. He closed his eyes and dozed. In his dream, he saw himself standing in a huge classroom. There were about six hundred desks in front of him. Behind him were blackboards covered with lists and lists of words—*cat, bat, fat, mat . . . could, should, would . . . split, quit, flit . . . soap, boat, moat . . . .* Josh pointed to the lists of words with a yardstick.

"So, as you can see," he said to the class, "reading and spelling are really very simple. There's nothing to be afraid of. With extra time, drill, and practice, you can read anything. You just have to learn the rules and practice. Most words follow the rules, except for the exceptions, and those you can look up in the dictionary or ask your teacher."

The students stamped their feet and clapped loudly. "Bravo, professor," shrieked a bearded man with a briefcase. Josh bowed and walked toward bright lights and movie cameras.

Sun streamed from the open window into Josh's eyes. He blinked and looked at the clock. The hour hand was past the nine.

"Is this a weekend?" Josh called to his mother.

"It's Saturday, Josh."

"Is *that* a weekend?"

"Yes. That's why I let you sleep late."

Josh sprang out of bed fully dressed and put on his baseball cap.

"I thought we'd agreed you would start laying out your clothes the night before, instead of wearing them to bed."

"Oh, Mom! It's easier this way."

"All right," said his mother, shaking her head, "but don't forget to clean your room." Josh pushed the Lego blocks under the bed. He put his dirty clothes back in the dresser drawer. He sprinkled birdseed into Gerbie's and Herbie's cage. Then he slid on his stomach to the bottom of the stairs.

While Josh waited for his toast to pop up, he heard voices. They seemed to be coming from the cellar. He walked to the top of the cellar stairs and listened.

"The president and the vice-president of the fishing club get to sit in lawn chairs. The rest of the members will have to sit on the floor."

"Yeah, and we can charge twenty-five cents dues each week. That way we can buy refreshments."

"Did your mom say you could come to Lake Winacchi with me?" Chomp, chomp. Josh recognized the click of Buck's chewing gum.

"Yeah, I can come. But there's one problem. Josh has to come, too."

"You're kidding! How come?"

He walked to the top of the cellar stairs and listened.

"My mom says that if we're going to set up the club-house in our cellar, Josh has to come fishing with us."

"Does that mean he's in our club?"

"No way. He has to be voted in by the officers just like everyone else."

"Yeah, and me and you are the officers!"

Josh smelled smoke. Quickly, he closed the cellar door. In the kitchen, flames shot from the toaster. He unplugged the cord and tried to pry the burned toast free with a fork. It crumbled. Josh tipped the toaster upside down and slammed it against the counter. Black toast crumbs covered the butter dish and fell to the floor. He decided to eat cereal for breakfast.

"Good heavens! What happened here?" asked his mother as she stopped in front of the toaster.

"I tried to clean the toaster for you," said Josh.

"Thanks, dear," she said, looking worried. "How about sweeping up the crumbs?"

"Okay, when I finish my cereal."

Josh went on chewing Cheerios with his mouth open. Milk dripped down his chin, and he wiped it off with his shirtsleeve. The best part about eating breakfast alone was not having to use good manners.

Footsteps sounded on the cellar stairs. Simon switched off the cellar light and came into the kitchen with Buck. "What a mess," he said, eyeing the crumbled toast.

"I'm making my breakfast," said Josh.

"Listen, you want to go fishing this afternoon?"

Josh slurped a bite of Cheerios. "Sure, where are you going?"

"We're going to a lake. It's pretty far away—miles."

"Is Mom driving you?"

"No, we're going on our bikes," Simon said. "You might be too young to make it."

"No, I'll go! Remind me to pack my new hooks." Simon looked annoyed.

"When are you leaving?" asked Josh.

"Right after lunch. You get to dig the worms. Buck and I will pack snacks. I'll bring the tackle box I got for camp."

Josh didn't mind digging worms. What he hated was getting the fish off the hook. The fish squirmed and looked pitiful. Putting your fingers into its slimy mouth was gross.

"Be ready at twelve-thirty sharp," said Simon.

"Okay. I'll put the worms in a can with dirt so they won't suffer."

"Oh, brother," said Simon, giving Buck a look.

Josh followed them out the kitchen door. He sat down in the middle of his mother's vegetable garden. Digging with a stick, he searched for worms.

The trip to Lake Winacchi took longer than Josh had expected. It wasn't like riding up to Gypsy Pond. That only took about fifteen minutes. This trip seemed more like hours. Buck led the way. They rode past Valley School and under the railroad bridge. Then they got to country roads. Buck said there was a faster route but it was too dangerous on Saturday. On Saturday all the traffic going to the shopping malls jammed the bigger roads.

"Hurry up," yelled Simon as Josh fell farther and farther behind.

"I'm going as fast as I can," Josh shouted back. Sweat ran down his neck. His heart was beating fast. They passed an apple orchard and two red barns. In front of the farmhouse a large German Shepherd was chained to a pole. It was sleeping in the sun.

"Wait up!" called Josh. At the end of the apple orchard he saw a fruit stand. Josh read the sign "Colb Cidre." His mouth watered. He felt in his pocket and pulled out his weekly allowance.

"How much longer?" Josh asked, as he paid for two more cups.

"Not much farther," Buck took a big gulp of cider. "The dirt road to the lake is just over that hill."

"That's not a hill, that's a mountain!" Josh's legs wobbled so, he could hardly stand.

"I knew you were too weak to make it," said Simon impatiently.

"I'm fine, just fine," said Josh.

They coasted down the hill and turned into the dirt road that led to Lake Winacchi.

Chapter 11

The parking lot at Lake Winacchi was jammed with cars, vans, and boat trailers. Families with babies and grandmothers sat at long picnic tables. The boys wheeled their bikes past the barbecue pit. They could smell roasting hot dogs in the humid air. Buck and Simon hitched their bikes together with a combination chain lock. Josh locked his bike to a pine tree.

"Let's get away from all these people," said Buck. "All those kids splashing around scare off fish. They feel underwater vibrations, you know." Chomp, chomp.

Josh limped along the lake trail behind Buck and his brother. He had a blister on his heel. His tongue felt like a potato chip, it was so dry. He wanted to lie down and rest. Finally, Buck stopped beside the water. "This is perfect," he announced. "No dogs or people to bother us," he said, unlatching the tackle box.

"Only mosquitos," said Simon, slapping his arm. "Let's eat our snack now before we start fishing."

Buck took out the canteen and crunch granola bars. He stuck his gum to a leaf while he ate. When he finished, he put the gum back into his mouth. Buck stabbed the worm with his hook. "I'm fishing over there," he said, pointing to a rock farther down the path. Simon baited his hook and followed Buck.

Josh gently eased the hook into the belly of his worm. He wanted it to suffer as little as possible. He threw the line into the lake. Using the knapsack as a pillow, Josh lay down in the leaves. He tied his fishing line to a stick and put it between his knees. If a fish yanked the line, it would wake him. He closed his eyes and imagined catching a sixteen-pound bass. It would be the biggest bass ever caught by a child under twelve in New Jersey history. He'd be in the newspapers. If that happened, they'd have to let him into the fishing club. He'd be too famous to be left out.

Josh woke up when he heard his brother's voice. "Look at this mama!" he shouted. He came racing down the path, a fish wriggling violently at the end of his fishing line. He dangled the dripping fish over Josh's head.

"Quit it!" cried Josh. He sat up and shivered. The sun had disappeared behind black clouds, and the wind whipped the tree leaves in sudden gusts. Josh looked across the water. The sailboats were gone. There were whitecaps on the lake.

"Looks like a thunderstorm," he said nervously. "Let's get out of here!"

"You're right," said Simon, as a roll of thunder echoed in the distance. "We probably should have left sooner. I thought the storm would blow over and miss us." Simon threw the hooks, lines, and sinkers back into the tackle box. Buck stuffed the fish into a plastic bag. They hurried down the winding path to their bikes.

The parking lot was deserted. The families had packed up their picnics and left. Only a black van remained, parked next to the barbecue pit.

"Look!" shrieked Buck. "They're stealing our bikes!"

"You're kidding!" Simon dropped his fish and tackle box. "Come on! Let's stop them!" He raced toward the van, followed by Buck and Josh. Buck didn't see the tree root. It was hidden in the leaves. He tripped and went sprawling to the ground.

"You okay?" Josh stopped and bent over Buck's body.

"My ankle," he groaned.

"Help!" yelled Simon. Josh stood up and raced toward his brother. He was clinging to the van door, fighting to pull it open. The driver lurched forward, flinging Simon to the ground. The van sped off down the rutted dirt road.

Josh squinted his eyes, trying to make out the license plate in the cloud of dust.

"706MBA. M-B-A. Mother Buys Apples," he said under his breath. He wrote 706 with a stick in the sand.

"What are you doing just standing there?" cried Simon rubbing his elbow. It was covered with blood.

"You all right, Simon?" asked Josh.

"Yeah, but what about Buck?" Simon asked. Buck lay limply in the leaves, his stomach heaving up and down.

Buck didn't see the tree root hidden in the leaves. He tripped and went sprawling to the ground.

"How do you feel?" asked Simon, kneeling beside his friend.

"I'm dizzy. Must have gotten the wind knocked out of me when I fell." Buck sat up and carefully felt his ankle. "I think I'm okay, except I swallowed my gum. How about your arm? Do you think you need stitches?"

"No way!" Simon dabbed the blood with a napkin from the trash can. "It stings but the bleeding's almost stopped."

Buck stood up. He winced with pain. "Ouch! It's getting worse. I must have sprained my ankle."

"I can't believe it," said Simon. "Those creeps just picked up our bikes in broad daylight and threw them in their van. They were still chained together!"

"My dad paid a lot of money for that bike," said Buck, rubbing his ankle. "He's going to kill me."

"I've been waiting for a ten-speed all my life," explained Simon.

"At least they didn't get *my* bike," said Josh. "It's lucky I chained it to a tree."

"Who'd want a dirt bike, anyway, when you can have two ten-speeds?" said Buck.

"Well, now what?" Simon said, still holding the napkin on his cut.

"Let's call home so Mom can come and pick us up in the car," suggested Josh. "Anyone got a quarter?"

Simon looked at Buck. Buck looked at Josh. Josh looked at his feet. "I spent all my allowance buying cider," he said.

"There goes that idea," said Simon. "Besides, there's no phone out here anyway."

Thunder rumbled nearby and raindrops began to fall. Buck limped toward a big tree. "Let's get out of the rain," he said, looking up at the thick branches.

"I'm not sitting under a tree in a thunderstorm," said Josh, "and I'd advise you not to pee."

"Who said anyone had to pee?" asked Simon. "You're such a dip. You're always trying to change the subject."

"See that canoe?" Buck pointed to a canoe lying next to a picnic table. "Let's turn it over and get under it, out of the storm."

Simon used his good arm to help Josh tip the canoe. They put a log at either end to raise it off the ground, so the canoe made a roof over their heads. They crept inside. It smelled musty, like damp life jackets. Simon put his fish on top of the tackle box and knapsack. Slowly, Buck unwrapped a fresh piece of gum and put it in his mouth. He tried to find a comfortable position.

"We've got to think of a plan," said Simon.

"I know one thing." Buck chewed, chomp, chomp. "I can't walk on this ankle." It was beginning to swell.

"We could just sit here until mom sends a search party out to find us," said Josh hopefully. "That way we wouldn't get wet if it rains."

"It's up to you, Josh," said Simon.

"What's up to me?"

"You've got to get help."

"Me! Why me?"

"Well, I hurt my arm and Buck hurt his ankle. Besides, you're the only one with a bike."

"But how can I find the way home? It's like miles away!" Josh felt his heart begin to pound.

"Here, I've got a map." Buck began to search through the knapsack. "I'll mark the route for you."

"I can't. I hate maps! I always read them wrong. Besides, I feel sick. I think my granola bar was rotten. I think I'm going to throw up."

"You'll be okay," said Simon. "You've got to go. We're depending on you!"

Buck pulled out a crumpled map and laid it on the grass. "See this blue?" he said, pointing to a blob about the size of a lima bean. "That's where we are. From here you go directly north."

"You mean I just go straight the whole way?"

"No, you dip!" sighed Simon. "North from where you are changes depending on which direction you're facing. He turned to Buck. "He'll go around in circles. He'll probably end up in another state!"

"Yeah, he's a real mental."

For a second Josh stared at the lake in angry silence. "That's it," he cried suddenly. "So you think I'm a mental! Well, you'll see! I'll show you, Buck. I'll show you good!" Josh crawled out from under the canoe. "You just watch me," he said, marching to his bike. Unlocking the chain, he hoisted himself onto the seat. He shook his fist. "And you, Simon, don't you *ever* call me a dip again!" he yelled. "You've teased me every single day since I was born. You think I'm such a wimp, huh? You'll see!" Josh swerved as he skidded in the soft sand of the parking lot. Then he took off down the dirt road, pedaling full speed.

"The map, Josh, wait! You forgot the map!" Simon ran after his brother, waving the map.

"I can do it myself," yelled Josh as he disappeared around the curve.

Chapter 12

Josh skidded to a stop. The dirt road from the lake ended with a bump. He remembered they had coasted down a hill just before turning into Lake Winacchi. He turned left and pedaled up the hill in the direction of the eerie sky.

At the crest, Josh stopped to rest his legs. He felt a drop of rain on his cheek, then another on his knee. A bolt of lightning zigzagged across the sky. Thunder shook the earth. Josh pedaled on against the wind. It came in gusts, pushing him back like an invisible shield.

Josh forced his bike on past the apple orchard. The fruit stand that sold apple cider had closed. Suddenly, like a bomb in a fireworks factory, thunder exploded around him. The storm was closer, much closer. "This is crazy," said Josh aloud. "Any minute I could get killed." He turned his bike around and headed back past the fruit stand toward the lake. I'll stay with Simon and Buck until the storm ends, he thought. Then go for help.

With the wind at his back, Josh glided toward the lake road. As he coasted downhill, he imagined his return. Simon would yell at him. He'd call him a dip and a wimp and a creep and a coward. He might not even let him back underneath the canoe. If Buck hadn't passed out with pain, he'd call him a retard and a mental. He'd probably punch him in the stomach.

Josh put on the brakes. He turned his bike around again. Slowly he started to pedal back up the hill. Already he felt exhausted. He panted hard. As he passed the apple stand, the rain became heavier. Huge drops, like frozen peas, bounced off the steaming pavement. Josh gripped the handlebars and pumped with all his strength.

Just ahead, he heard a tree branch snap. It crashed into the road. Josh swerved to avoid it. Coming directly at him were the blinding headlights of a car. He veered right and rode into a ditch. The car sped past. He didn't even see me, thought Josh. That car could have run me over. I could be lying in the road bleeding to death.

Josh gritted his teeth and went on. Farther down the road, he saw a blinking yellow light. At the intersection, he got off his bike and waited for a car to stop.

"Please!" Josh waved his arms at a sports car. "Which way to Ledgewood?" he yelled. The driver opened his window a crack. "Go left, then make your next right onto Sheraton Road, go about one hundred yards and turn right onto Godwin. Follow Godwin until...."

"Thanks," said Josh, as he sunk into the wet grass.

He didn't care if he sat in mud. A heart-pounding panic bubbled up inside him. He could even taste it in his mouth. Panic had a bitter taste, like chewing grown-up aspirin. He realized he didn't remember one word the driver had said.

Lightning crackled down the sky. In the sudden light, he saw the farmhouse beyond the two red barns. Josh got back on his bike and pedaled toward it. He would sit inside the cozy kitchen until the storm passed. He would drink ice-cold Coke and call his mother on the telephone. As Josh got closer, he heard the sharp bark of a dog. The German Shepherd paced the ground, howling at the thunder. It looked like a police attack dog, the kind that's trained to sink its jagged teeth into human flesh. Josh pedaled past the farmhouse.

Farther down the road, Josh braked at a four-way STOP sign. He waved his arms at an oncoming car. It sped past, splattering him with mud. Another car approached the intersection. A lady with white hair rolled down her window.

"Do you need help?" she asked.

"Which way to Ledgewood?" Josh tried to make his voice sound calm, as if it were normal to bike through lightning.

"Take a left here, and then your next right. At Godwin, bear right and continue past Phil's Apple Farm until you get to. . . ." Josh stopped paying attention. He knew he couldn't remember so many directions. "Go left, go left," he repeated. "Thanks," he added, feeling for the wart on his left thumb.

"Keep going, keep going," he chanted to himself, "or you're a dip forever."

"Does your mother know you're out here?" asked the lady.

"Sure!" said Josh, trying to smile.

The lady shook her head. "I don't know what's wrong with parents these days, letting children ride around in a storm like this. They ought to be arrested." She drove away, still shaking her head.

Josh turned left and pedaled down the road. "Keep going," he said to himself. "Give up and you're a dip for life. Keep going." He said it over and over.

"Want a ride, kid?" A man in a pickup truck pulled up next to Josh.

"No, thanks. Just tell me which road to take for Ledgewood."

"You're a long way off, kid," said the man. He had bad breath like he'd been drinking whiskey. "Sure you don't want a lift?" He took a drink of something hidden in a paper bag. "We could put your bike in the back of my truck."

"I'm not allowed to ride with strangers," called Josh, still pedaling.

"Okay, kid, follow this road until you come to a STOP sign, turn right off Godwin onto Forest Avenue and then . . . ."

"Thanks," yelled Josh, repeating the first direction under his breath. At the STOP sign he turned right.

Car wheels threw up blinding sprays of water. Josh could taste it on his lips, a muddy, oily taste. He'd never seen it rain so hard, not since Hurricane David. On the left, Josh recognized the school with the jungle gym made of truck tires. "I'm not lost yet," he said as he swerved to avoid another giant puddle.

For the first time since he left the lake, Josh came to a sidewalk. He did a wheelie up over the curb. His wet clothes clung to his body. He didn't feel cold even though the temperature had dropped. "Keep going . . . keep going, keep going, or you're a dip forever," he chanted to himself. He lowered his body to the handlebars and pedaled like he was coming in first in a World Cup bike race.

Josh read the sign at the next crossroads. It said LEDGEWOOD with an arrow pointing left. Josh pushed the wet hair out of his eyes and watched for tree root cracks in the sidewalk. He pedaled past the town hospital. He wanted to go in the emergency room to have his pulse checked, but he remembered Buck and Simon and kept on.

At the Exxon gas station, Josh asked the way to Chestnut Street. He listened for the first direction and blocked out the rest. At the YMCA he asked a mailman which street to take next. As he coasted under the railroad bridge, Josh felt a rush of relief. He knew where he was! He recognized Hal's Pharmacy and the store where you could buy *Playboy* and bubble gum. It was only about five minutes more to his house and to his mom and dad.

Chapter 13

Josh pushed his bike up the steep gravel driveway. His feet squished inside his waterlogged sneakers. His legs were trembling. He slipped off his shoes and left them on the back porch. His mother heard the kitchen screen door slam.

"Josh, I've been so worried! Where have you been?" Josh could tell she would have hugged him if he hadn't been dripping wet.

"Buck's hurt and so is Simon." Josh panted. "We were at the lake fishing and—"

"Are you okay, Josh? You're covered with mud!"

"I'm fine, Dad. We've got to drive back and get them. Hurry!"

"What happened? Why didn't you all ride home together?"

"Two guys stole their bikes and Simon hurt his arm and Buck broke his ankle and—"

"Where are they now?"

"Underneath a canoe."

"Underneath a canoe?" screeched his mother. "Don't tell me you were in a canoe without a grownup."

"No, Mom. We didn't go *in* the canoe. We went

under the canoe to get away from the thunderstorm."

"But how did you get home?"

Josh leaned against the sink in case his legs collapsed.

"I biked home all by myself."

"You can't be serious . . . by yourself? All the way from Lake Winacchi?"

"I almost got hit by lightning four times."

His mother gasped. "You mean you were biking alone in that terrible thunderstorm?"

"It was my resiponsility."

"Your responsibility?"

"Yeah. Buck and Simon were counting on me."

Mr. Grant pulled the car keys out of his back jean pocket. "Susan, I"ll go get the boys. You get Josh cleaned up."

"I want to come too, Dad!"

Mr. Grant put his hand on Josh's shoulder. "I guess you deserve to do exactly what you want, young man. Run upstairs and change."

"But Ben, he's so wet and exhausted. He'll catch his death of cold."

"If he's strong enough to bike home from Lake Winacchi, he's strong enough to fight off a cold!"

Josh changed into a warm flannel shirt and jeans. He threw his muddy clothes into the bathtub. Then he grabbed his raincoat and wet sneakers and ran out to the car.

"Bye, Mom," he called as the screen door slammed behind him.

Strokes of afternoon sun began to appear in the clearing sky. The storm had blown away the sticky, humid heat. The air felt cool and fresh, like a blanket had been lifted off the state of New Jersey.

Josh fell asleep in the front seat of the car. He woke up when his father swerved abruptly to avoid a deep puddle.

"Park here, Dad," said Josh nervously. "If we go any closer we'll get stuck in the mud for sure."

"Is that the canoe over there?" asked Mr. Grant, pulling the car off the road.

"Yeah! That's it!" Josh jumped out of the car and raced toward the lake, his father close behind him. "Simon, I made it!" he yelled. There was no answer. "Are you there?" Josh peered under the canoe. It was empty. No one was there. He scratched his head. "I wonder where they went."

Just then they heard a branch snap in the woods, and Simon came running through the trees. "You made it!" He hugged Josh. "I thought you'd never get here." Then he hugged his dad. "Come quick! Buck's in a lot of pain. It was so uncomfortable under the canoe that I moved him into the woods after the storm blew over."

They followed Simon through the wet bushes. "Let's see your arm, son," said Mr. Grant, staring at the dried blood. "Looks like a mean scrape."

"Don't worry about me, Dad. It's Buck who needs help." Buck lay shivering in a soggy bed of damp leaves. "I covered him with newspapers from the trash can to keep him warm."

"Sure glad to see you," Buck said, forcing a smile. "My ankle is really killing me."

Mr. Grant and Josh helped Buck hop to the car. Carefully, they eased him into the front seat. Simon got the knapsack, tackle box, and dead fish, and climbed into the back with Josh.

"We'll go directly to the emergency room for x-rays," said Mr. Grant, starting the car. "We can call your parents from the hospital."

Buck winced. He rubbed his swollen ankle. "It hurts," he said.

"You boys had quite a day!" said Mr. Grant.

"You can say that again!" Simon looked at Josh. "How'd you make it home?"

"No problem," said Josh.

"I can't believe it! I thought we'd never see you again."

"The storm was pretty bad. I almost got struck by lightning five times."

Buck turned around and stared at Josh in amazement. "You mean you kept riding even in that thunderstorm?"

"Had to. You were depending on me."

"Me and Simon decided that if you got help we'd make you an officer of the fishing club. You can choose secretary or treasurer. President and vice-president are already taken."

"You mean I can be in your club?" Josh asked in surprise.

"You're not just *in* our club. You're an officer!"

Josh turned to his brother. "Give me five," he said,

slapping Simon's hands. "I can't be secretary. My handwriting is too crooked. Besides, I can't spell. What does a treasurer do?"

"He takes care of the money," said Simon.

"Then I'll be treasurer. I always add better when I'm counting money." Josh stared out the window. He pictured himself sitting at a table with stacks of dollar bills in front of him. All the kids in the neighborhood would bring him money. He'd collect it every day after school. He'd keep it in a safe in the clubhouse. No one would know the combination of the safe, not even Simon.

"After we take Buck to the hospital, we have another stop to make," said his father.

"What's that?" Josh asked.

"We've got to go to the police station and report the stolen bikes."

Josh had never been to the police station before. He wondered if it would have a jail.

"Can we go out for pizza tonight?" asked Josh. "I'm starving."

"Sure, Josh," said his father, "this is a special night."

Chapter 14

The police station was on the first floor of the Ledgewood Town Hall. An officer in a blue uniform sat behind a desk. He sipped coffee from a mug with an American flag on the front.

"We'd like to report two stolen bikes," Simon said to the officer.

"Were they inspected and registered here in Ledgewood?" asked the officer.

"Yeah. I mean, yes, sir."

"Do you have the inspection numbers?"

Simon pulled a slip of paper out of his pocket. "I've got the number for one bike. I don't know my friend's number, though. He's in the hospital. He's with his parents getting an x-ray."

"Was he attacked by the perpetrator?"

"No, he tripped. He'll be all right. He just wants his bike back."

"I don't blame him." The officer put on his eyeglasses. "I'll need some information, son. When did you discover the bikes missing?"

"The bikes got stolen about three o'clock this afternoon from the parking lot next to Lake Winacchi."

"If you kids would learn to lock your bikes, this sort of thing wouldn't happen so often." The officer leaned back in his chair and took another sip of coffee.

"But we *did* lock them! We chained the two front tires together. Then we saw these guys dump the two bikes into a van and drive away."

"Can you describe the van?"

"Yes, sir, it was black with a sunset painted on the back."

"Did you get the license plate number?"

"No, sir."

"Wait a minute," Josh interrupted. "I think I remember the license."

"Wait a minute," Josh interrupted. "I think I remember the license." He closed his eyes and tried to picture the number he'd written in the sand.

"It was a New Jersey plate and the number was 7... 0... 6... Mother Buys Apples."

"What?"

"Mother Buys Apples. M.B.A. That's a mnemonic device I learned in school to help remember things."

"Well, I'll be!" said the officer, smoothing his bald head.

"That's mnemonic, with a silent *m*." Josh could tell

that Simon was impressed. The police officer wrote the number down on a slip of paper. "If you'll wait just a minute," he said, "I'll go check this out."

Simon walked over to the drinking fountain and gulped quick sips of water. Mr. Grant sat down on a wooden bench in the waiting area. Josh sat down beside him, and rested his head against his father's shoulder. His dad put one arm around him and hugged him close. Josh sat up straight when the police officer returned.

"I'm sorry but there's no van listed in New Jersey with this license plate number," he announced.

Josh scratched his head. "Wait a minute!" he cried. "I've got it! Sometimes I mix up letters like *w* and *m*. Maybe the number is 706WBA."

Simon returned from the water fountain. He shifted his feet and began to explain to the officer: "You see, my brother is learning disabled. That doesn't mean he's stupid or anything like that. It just means he needs special help to learn things like reading and math."

"I know just what you mean. My grandson, Tommy, has the same problem. Let me check out 706WBA. You could be right. That's just the sort of mistake Tommy would make."

The officer returned, holding a pad of paper. "This time you're absolutely correct," he said, adjusting his glasses. "That van is registered to a man in Lawngreen, New Jersey. We might get your bikes back after all, thanks to this young man's memory." The officer patted Josh on the head. "Smart boys you've got here," he said to Mr. Grant as he finished filling out the forms. "I'll call you when I have information to report."

On the way home in the car, Simon asked his father if they could stop at the Biddlemans' house. Buck and Kelly were sitting on the front porch. Buck had his leg up on a footstool. He was reading a fishing magazine and drinking soda from a can, a pair of crutches propped on the wall behind him.

"What happened at the hostipal?" cried Josh, climbing the porch stairs.

"The x-ray said I broke my ankle. I've got to wear this dumb cast until Thanksgiving."

"Does it still hurt?"

"Not too bad. You want to sign my cast?" Kelly went inside and brought out her collection of Magic Markers. "What color do you want?" she asked, handing Simon the box. Simon picked out a red marker and wrote "Good Luck, Simon G." on the cast.

Josh picked out a lime green marker. "This time I'll be careful," he said.

"Careful about what?" asked Buck.

"Careful not to write the *J* backward."

Mr. Grant turned to Josh. "Tell Buck what happened about the license number at the police station."

"I'll tell it," said Simon. "The policeman asked for the license of the van and—"

"No, *I'll* tell it!" said Josh. He stepped in front of his brother.

"You see, when these two guys drove away with the bikes, we didn't know what to do. . . ." The screen door opened and Mr. and Mrs. Biddleman stepped onto the front porch. They sat down next to Buck.

"Go on, Josh," said Mr. Grant. He smiled proudly at his son.

Josh looked anxiously at Simon. "You tell," he said.

"No, you tell. You were the one who lived through it."

"Well, since Buck and Simon were both injured," Josh took a deep breath, "and I had the only bike, I had to go all by myself in the storm back to get help at my house. I went in the pouring rain. I almost got hit by lightning *six* times!"

Kelly's eyes bulged wide open. "Boy, that's scary. How did you ever know what roads to go on?"

"I didn't. But I remembered lots of landmarks we passed going to the lake, like the farm with a terrible dog and the railroad bridge, and other stuff like that. Sometimes I stopped cars and asked people which way to go."

"Tell about getting our bikes back," said Simon.

"You're kidding! We're getting our bikes back?" Buck looked thrilled.

"Well, I remembered the license plate of the van because I wrote it in the sand and I said it over and over in my brain. Only I mixed it up but I remembered it after I figured out how it got mixed up."

"Oh," said Buck.

"Buckie sure would like his bike back," said Mrs. Biddleman.

"If you do get your bike back, can I ride it until

you get your cast off?" Kelly asked, chewing on the end of her pigtails.

"I'll think about it." Buck rubbed his fingers down the bumpy cast.

"Please! I'm big enough for a ten-speed."

"Well, I guess so," he said glumly.

"Hope you feel better, Buck," said Mr. Grant. "We've got to get home. Susan will be worried about the boys. Besides, I promised to take the family to a pizza place for supper—in honor of Josh!"

"Thanks for stopping by," said Buck. "Hey, Josh, wait up." Buck hobbled toward him. "I gotta thank you for all you did, getting help and everything. You were cool, man. I mean it. Real brave."

"No problem." Josh waved and jumped down the porch steps. "I call front seat by the window," he yelled to Simon as they raced toward the car.

"No way, dip, it's my turn!"

"You promised not to call me dip, 'member?"

"Oh, sorry," said Simon climbing in the back seat.

On the way home they passed a group of Simon's friends organizing a game of kickball in Citizen's Park. Mr. Grant stopped the car.

"Want to play?" yelled the tall kid with mushroom ears.

Simon stuck his head out the back seat window. "Not tonight," he yelled.

"How come you're not playing?" asked Josh as the car pulled away from the curb.

"Because we've got more important things to do,

that's why. We've got to start setting up the fishing club. Mom says we can use the whole cellar. So far, everyone we've asked wants to join."

"Can Kip and David be in the club too?"

"Yeah, sure, Josh."

Josh lifted his left foot onto the front seat and retied his shoe. He imagined what it would be like, being treasurer. He'd put his money collecting table right next to the washing machine. In between club meetings, he could hide his safe in the clothes dryer. A robber would never look in a dryer for money. He imagined how he'd tell the club about going to Lake Winacchi. He'd tell them how he saved Buck and Simon. Everyone would listen to him, even girls.

"You boys go wash up," said Mr. Grant as he put on the brakes at the top of the driveway. "I'll get your mother. She'll be delighted to eat out for a change."

"Me, too," nodded Josh. "Pizza is the best food in America."

Chapter 15

Simon held the screen door at the pizza restaurant open for his mother.

"Thanks, dear," she said as she slid into a booth. "You boys must be hungry."

"Mom, I'm starving," said Josh. "Me and Simon—"

"Simon and I," corrected his mother. "Go on, you and Simon...."

"Simon and me are going to sweep and dust the cellar for our club."

"What club?"

"Our fishing club." Simon picked up a menu. "And today, at the lake, we voted Josh treasurer."

"That's wonderful! Congratulations, Josh!"

"I've got more good news," said Mr. Grant. "While you boys were gone, we had a phone call from Mrs. Mantimer."

"You did? What did she say?" asked Josh anxiously.

"She said you're a great kid!"

"And a smart one," added his mother.

"She said that once you learn to compensate for your learning problems, you'll be definite college material." Dad looked pleased.

"What's *constipate* mean?" Josh asked.

"Compensate means you learn how to deal with your problem," Mom explained. "For example, if you're a bad speller you get to be really zippy at looking up words in the dictionary."

Mr. Grant leaned over across the table. He mussed Josh's hair. "Nice going!" he said proudly.

"I know what I want to order," announced Simon. "I'd like lasagna and a large Coke with no ice with a side order of spaghetti."

"How about you, Josh?" Mom asked.

"I'd like three slices of pepperoni pizza with extra cheese and a Coke with no ice and a salad with no cucumbers, please."

"Are you sure you can eat all that?"

"Sure, Mom. I biked about twenty miles today, don't forget."

The waitress brought the two Cokes and a bottle of red wine. She had on blue eye makeup and long dangling earrings with feathers at the end. Simon pulled a comb out of his back pocket.

"Don't comb your hair at the table, Simon," whispered his mother. "It's not polite."

"By the way, Josh, you had two phone calls. One was from a girl who said–"

"A girl? Are you kidding, Mom?" asked Simon. "A girl called Josh?"

"Yes. You're invited to her birthday party, Josh," Mom went on. "She said you're in her art class."

"No kidding!" said Josh, gulping his Coke. "Who else called?"

"Somebody named David. He wants you to come for a sleepover."

"I know him. He's in my class."

"Of course you know him, dip. You think a complete stranger would invite you to a sleepover?"

"I thought you promised never to call me dip again."

"I can't help it." Simon grinned. "I can't stop. I'll try to cut back though, to like just ten or twelve times a day."

"Gee, thanks!" said Josh, smiling. "You're a real pal!"

After dinner, Mr. Grant drove home the long way. There was a September chill in the air. Josh curled up next to Simon in the back seat and fell asleep. Simon put his sweatshirt over Josh's legs to keep him warm.

"Run upstairs and get washed up," said Mrs. Grant as she unlocked the back door. Bugs swarmed around the porch light. Josh quickly slammed the screen door behind him.

In the bathroom, Josh pulled mint dental floss between his two new front teeth. He washed his face and hands and hung the damp washcloth over the side of the bathtub to dry.

"Come kiss me goodnight," he called to his mother. He laid out his clean clothes for the next morning, and put on his pajamas. Then he sprinkled birdseed into the cage for Gerbie and Herbie and climbed under the covers.

There was a note in Simon's handwriting.

"Want to do your twenty minutes of reading tonight?" Mom put her soft hand up his pajama top and began to rub his back.

"No way."

"What were your best and worst moments today?"

Josh knew his mother would say that. She asked the same question every night. Josh sat up in bed.

"My worst moment was when I was under the canoe. I was scared to stay there and I was scared to leave. I thought I was going to throw up! And my best moment was...," Josh paused and slid back down under the covers, "my best moment was when Dad drove me back to the lake and I got to prove to Buck and Simon that I made it alive."

"Dad and I are proud of you."

"Simon thought I'd ride my bike into another state. Maybe he thought I'd be hit by lightning and lost forever."

"He told me he was really worried about you."

"He did?"

"He said even Buck was worried."

"No kidding?"

"Simon asked me to give this to you." Josh watched as his mother took an envelope out of her skirt pocket. Inside he found two dimes, four nickles, and ten pennies. There was a note in Simon's handwriting.

DUES FOR FISHING CLUB
$.25 BUCK $.25 KELLY
I LOVE YOU DIP
        SIMON

Josh put the envelope under his pillow. "I'll put this in the clothes dryer tomorrow," he mumbled. He felt his mom's soft lips on his cheek. He didn't see her tiptoe out of the bedroom. He was already fast asleep.

A Note to My Readers

You might want to read this part of the book with your mom or dad. This part is also great for kids without learning disabilities. In it I'll answer questions that learning disabled children have asked me.

"Is There Something Wrong with my Brain?"

Why do some smart kids have so much trouble learning? This is an important question to answer. Many people are studying the cause of learning problems. They are studying different parts of that giant computer in your head—the brain.

Josh secretly felt he was retarded. He thought his brain was broken or damaged. He didn't understand how he could try so hard and be such a "dud" in school. Learning disabled people are *different*. They are different in the way their brains take in, organize, and send out messages. They can see and hear and feel and move just like everyone else. Like some people, they show a "gap" between their potential (what they *could* do) and their performance (what they *are* doing), but unlike most, they have greater difficulty doing certain things in certain ways. They must find other ways to accomplish the same goals. This gap shows up in their schoolwork, and sometimes in the way they get along with other kids. Instead of thinking of your brain as damaged, think of it as different.

Question: What do all these people have in common? Leonardo Da Vinci (artist), Hans Christian Andersen (storyteller), Bruce Jenner (Olympic gold medalist), Agatha Christie (mystery writer), Albert Einstein (mathematician), Henry "the Fonz" Winkler (actor), and Tom Cruise (actor).

Answer: Each one was learning disabled and *outstanding* in his field.

"How Do I Know if I Have a Learning Disability?"

There are many words or labels that tell that a person has a "learning difference." Some of these labels are "learning disabled," "dyslexic," "minimally brain damaged," "perceptually impaired," and "neurologically impaired." These labels tell us that children have special needs. Like Josh, they learn best with special help.

Every single "L.D." (learning disabled) child is different. Some have one or two symptoms. Others have ten or twelve symptoms. See if you or any of your friends have problems like those that follow.

Short Attention Span

You can't keep your mind on your work. You are bothered by the sound of the pencil sharpener, or the ticking of the clock, or a fly buzzing by the window. You think about baseball during a math lesson. You draw monsters all over your workbook covers. The teacher keeps telling you, "Stop daydreaming and pay attention!"

Disorganized

Your school desk is a mess. Your dad says your bedroom looks like a rat's nest. You can't find your assignment book. You leave your jacket at the playground. You forget where you left your lunch box. Your mom says that if your head weren't attached to your body, you'd lose it.

Mixups in Time and Space

You can't remember what day comes after Wednesday. Jigsaw puzzles drive you crazy. When you color, it's hard to keep the Magic Marker inside the lines. You get lost going to the mailbox. You can't remember if Boston is north or south. You think the month of May comes in the fall, after October. You have trouble copying words from the blackboard. When you set up your paper heading, the words come out spaced all wrong.

Overactive

You can't sit still. You wriggle your feet and fidget with your pencil. In class you get in and out of your seat. You get kids' attention by acting silly. You wish you could jump over desks instead of sitting at them. At the dinner table, you tip back in your chair and spill your milk. The babysitter tells your mom you're hyperactive. Your teacher picks on you and tells you twenty times a day to sit down and stay still. You want to be a movie stunt man when you grow up.

Underactive

You'd rather watch than play at recess. When the teacher yells at the class, you think she's only mad at you. You've decided that everyone in the class is smarter and better looking than you. Your teacher says you are quiet, sensitive, and very cooperative. You learn ways to keep people from discovering that you're stupid. Your report card makes you feel ashamed. You keep a locked diary where no one will see your bad spelling. Sometimes in school you wish you could become invisible.

Problems with Your Family

Your parents think you're lazy. Your sister says you act like a "baby" and a "creep." You often lose your temper and act before you think. You feel your parents love their other kids more than they love you. You lose your bookbag and make everyone late for school. Your grandfather wants you to go to Harvard. You can't get the right words out at the dinner table. Your mom won't let you cross streets alone or ride your bike downtown. You wish you could say the right things at the right time like your sister.

Memory Problems

You forget what the teacher tells you to do. You can't remember what a word looks like after the blackboard is erased. You forget your best friend's telephone number. You say "what?" about fifty times a day. Every time you play Monopoly, you forget the rules. When the principal comes in, you can't remember his name. You say "the thing that goes buzz in the morning" because common words like *alarm clock* suddenly fall out of your head.

Problems in Reading

You lose your place. You skip words and lines. You mix up letters that look alike (*b, p, d* and *m, n, w*). You read *saw* for *was* and *quite* for *quiet*. You think the words *pin* and *pim* sound alike. When you sound out the word *hat*, you still have to sound out *mat, bat,* and *fat*. You know a word one day and forget it the next. You get confused between what happened in the beginning, middle, or end of a story. You hate to read out loud. You never read for pleasure unless your parents force you.

Problems in Spelling and Writing

You can spell a word on Thursday night and forget it by Friday's test. You can't remember if the word *home* is spelled *hoom, hoem, howm,* or *hoam*. Your handwriting is terrible. When you print, the letters are crooked and spaced too close or too far apart. Even when you write your best, the teacher tells you to copy it over. You have good ideas but you just can't seem to get them down on paper.

Problems in Math

You used to write all the numbers backwards. You confuse 19 and 91. You put numbers in the wrong columns. In word problems, you never know if you should add or subtract. You remember 6 + 8 = 14 one day and forget it the next. Your homework papers are crumpled and full of eraser smudges. You hate workbook pages with "bigger than–less than" examples. You do better if you have a number line to look at or popsicle sticks to count.

Problems in Gym

You trip over your own feet. You're the first to fall off the balance beam. When the teacher says turn left, you go right. The captain picks you last for the baseball team. When you swing on the ropes you get dizzy. You wish you could be the best at *something*.

Remember, every L.D. child is different. You might have beautiful handwriting and still show signs of a learning difference. Bruce Jenner *never* fell off the balance beam. He says one reason he became an outstanding athlete was because of his learning problems. It was a lot easier to be great on the playing field than it was inside the classroom.

"What Does It Feel Like
To Be Learning Disabled?"

If you blindfold your eyes, you can sense what it is like to be blind. If you plug up your ears, you can sense what it is like to be deaf. A learning difference is more difficult to imagine. Sometimes it is called the "invisible handicap." This exercise will give you some idea of what it feels like to have a learning disability.

1. Find a pencil and a piece of paper.
2. Stand in front of a mirror.
3. Put the paper against your forehead.
4. Looking into the mirror, write the word *good*.
5. Look at the word. Did you write it correctly?
6. Try again!

Now pretend that the teacher is standing next to you. "Hurry up!" she says. "Everyone else is finished!" No matter how smart you are or how hard you are trying, you can't do it right.

Think of your brain as a giant computer. Like a machine, it sometimes has bad connections. A short circuit comes if the brain gets "overloaded." It gets overloaded when too many messages come in at once from your eyes, ears, nose, and fingers. These messages get confused. You wish you had a fine tuning knob behind your ear to bring things back into focus.

For L.D. children, this "brain scramble" shows up in many ways. It shows in thinking, reading, writing, and talking. Remember how Josh wrote *no* for *on* and read *saw* for *was*? He also confused the order of letters in words, like *ostipit* for *opposite*, and words in sentences like *Where you are going?* You can imagine how frustrating it is to read, write, and talk with "brain scramble." No wonder some L.D. kids think they are stupid or crazy.

Other common word mixups are:

aminal for *animal*	*hostipal* for *hospital*
pisgetti for *spaghetti*	*engle mushin* for *English muffin*

"Do Many People Have Learning Problems?"

Experts think that one person in every ten has learning problems. That means 10 percent of the population of the United States has a learning difference — about twenty-five million people! Most experts think the problem runs in certain families. Boys are affected three to four times more often than girls. Very few Oriental children have learning disabilities.

Ask your father or grandfather or great-aunt if they had trouble learning. Perhaps you have relatives or classmates with a learning difference.

"Can You Test to Find a Learning Difference?"

If you are sick, you go to the doctor. The doctor might do tests to find out how to make you feel better. School tests do the same thing. They help your teachers know the best way to teach you. Achievement tests show your strengths and weaknesses. Perceptual tests show your learning style. These tests are used to help you, your parents, and your teachers understand your "learning difference."

What is a "learning style?" Some kids remember a new word by how it looks. They picture, in their minds, the size and shape of the letters. They have a strong *visual* learning style. Other children remember a new word by how it sounds. They blend together the sound of the letters. They remember, in their minds, what they hear. They have a strong *auditory* learning style.

Some children learn best when the visual and the auditory parts of the brain work together. This *multisensory* way of teaching is good for children with a learning disability. When a child can see, say, and write a word all at once, it helps the brain remember.

Teachers can help structure learning by breaking information down into tiny pieces. Step by step, each piece of information is introduced in a logical sequence. When a child has learned one step, he is ready to advance to the next step. In this way teaching is based on a solid ladder of success, not failure. Children with a learning difference *do* learn. It just takes extra time, effort, and organization.

Many learning disabled children are poor test-takers. They work slowly. Often they do not finish the test. "Brain-overload" might come if there are too many words, pictures, or numbers on a page. Teachers are finding new ways to test L.D. children. They give spoken tests instead of written tests. They give L.D. kids extra time and support. In this way, the test shows better what an L.D. child really knows. Tests are one of the many tools used to find and help a child with a learning difference.

"What Should I Do When Kids Tease Me?"

Think about how you act with other children. Is there something you do that "turns them off?" Do you act silly or tough or babyish or bossy? Do you lose your temper quickly? Are you so shy that they can't really get to know you?

Some kids are very sensitive to other people's feelings. Other children seem unaware of people's "vibes" or unspoken messages. They find it hard to make friends with kids and grownups. Without meaning to, they say and do the wrong thing at the wrong moment. This behavior can even make friends look for someone else to play with.

If you feel picked on or left out, tell someone about it. A teacher or your parents can help you think up new strategies – different ways to act. One strategy or plan might be to talk to the kids who are bothering you. Tell them how you feel and what makes you upset. If you change and they change, everyone will probably feel a lot happier.

"Sometimes I Think My Family Doesn't Understand Me!"

It is not easy for a child to have a learning disability. It is also not easy for the family. Some families don't want to admit that there is a problem. They might say their child is doing poorly in school because he is "so smart he is bored." Other families try to protect their child. They know there is a problem but they don't talk about it. They don't want their child to feel different. They tend to give the child special privileges, like fewer jobs around the house.

Sometimes families get upset, angry, and frustrated. They call the child "uncooperative" and "lazy." Remember when Simon called his brother a "learning-disabled dummy?" He had mixed feelings about his brother. At times, he stood up for him. At other times he felt embarrassed by Josh's behavior. If family, friends, and neighbors know about learning problems, they will learn to show special understanding.

How you think your family feels about you is very important. If your family can be open and honest about feelings, it helps. Talk about anger, hurt feelings, jealousy, and what makes you laugh. Talk about how it feels to have a learning disability. You will learn better in school if you know your family is standing strongly behind you.

"Will I Ever Be a Good Reader and Get Good Grades in School?"

The answer to that question is up to you! A learning difference never really goes away. You learn to live with it. You learn to compensate. That means you figure out ways to learn in spite of the problem. Josh was compensating when he looked for the wart on his left thumb. He coped with the problem by finding his own solution to which was his right and left hand.

Your family and the school will work together to give you a good education. The I.E.P. (Individualized Educational Plan) tells about your needs and strengths. It sets goals that are not too hard or too easy for you to reach. There are now laws that protect children with learning disabilities. One of these laws says that a child must be in the "least restrictive environment."

The least restrictive environment is most often the regular classroom where you get special help. Teachers these days get training to teach children with learning differences. Your parents and the school will decide the best class for you.

Experts are working hard to find out more about learning disabilities. They are doing research to find out what causes a learning difference. They are also looking for ways to prevent and treat learning problems. Doctors are studying how certain medicine affects learning in the brain. Teachers are using computers and new "multisensory" teaching methods.

It is important to spot a learning difference early. It is never too soon or too late to help a person with a learning disability.

Children with a learning disability *can* grow up to be good readers and get good grades in school. They can be creative and productive and successful. If you have a learning difference, you can teach your brain to work better and better. For that hard work and special courage, you deserve congratulations!

If you would like more information about learning disabilities, write or call these organizations.

Learning Disabilities
  Association of America (LDA)
4156 Library Road
Pittsburgh, PA 15234
Telephone: (412) 341-1515
Internet: www.ldanatl.org

Orton Dyslexia Society (ODS)
Chester Building
8600 La Salle Road, Suite 382
Baltimore, MD 21204
Telephone: (410) 296-0232
Internet: http://ods.org

The Council for
  Exceptional Children
1920 Association Drive

Reston, VA 22091-1589
Telephone: (800) 328-0272
Internet: www.cec.sped.org

National Center for
  Learning Disabilities
381 Park Avenue South
Suite 1401
New York, NY 10016
Telephone: (212) 545-7510
Internet: www.ncld.org

LD OnLine:
Box 2626
Washington, DC 20013
Telephone: (703) 998-2800
Internet: www.ldonline.org

About the Author

CAROLINE JANOVER grew up with a learning difference in a small town in New Hampshire. Her second year in the second grade, she invented her own private language and began to write nightly in locked diaries. As the mother of two bright, creative, dyslexic sons, Caroline now weaves real-life experiences into fiction as she writes about the triumphs of young people who struggle to pay attention and to learn in school. Caroline is also the author of *The Worst Speller in Jr. High* (Free Spirit Publishing: Minneapolis, MN 1995) and *Zipper: The Boy with ADHD* (Woodbine House, Bethesda, MD 1997).

A graduate of Sarah Lawrence College, Caroline received Master's Degrees from Boston University and Fairleigh Dickinson University. She currently lives with her husband in Ridgewood, NJ where she is a Learning Disabilities Teacher/Consultant in the public school system. A recipient of the Governor's Outstanding Teacher Award, Caroline lectures nationally to children, parents and teachers about the perceptual problems and creative strengths of children with ADHD and dyslexia.

Special Issues for Kids!

LET'S TALK TRASH
The Kids' Book About Recycling
Kelly McQueen and David Fassler, M.D.

Children hear about oil spills, rain forests, and recycling on television and in school. They worry about the earth and personally feel the effects of pollution when a favorite beach is closed in the summer. *Let's Talk Trash* presents the problem of solid waste disposal for further thought and discussion among young children, their teachers or their parents.

"As a former teacher, I highly recommend this creative introduction to an important contemporary topic." **—Constance Fornier, Ph.D., Texas A&M University**

"Never has 'talking trash' been so much fun! This book takes a refreshing look at a tough problem. I hope kids will share this book with their parents so that we all understand why it's important to protect our beautiful environment."
—Madeleine M. Kunin, Governor of Vermont

$14.95 paperback, $18.95 plastic comb spiral
Ages 4-10. 168 pages. Illustrated by children.

WHAT'S A VIRUS ANYWAY?
The Kids' Book About AIDS

David Fassler, M.D. and Kelly McQueen

AIDS can be a difficult subject to discuss with young children. However, children hear a lot about the disease at a very early age. *What's a Virus, Anyway?* is a simple introduction to help adults talk with children. The book includes children's drawings and questions, and provides basic information in a manner appropriate for 4-10 year olds.

"...that people with AIDS are just like everyone else, makes this book particularly distinctive." **—Booklist**

$8.95 paperback, $12,95 plastic comb spiral
Ages 4-10. 70 pages. Illustrated by children.

Also, now a new Spanish edition:
¿QUE ES UN VIRUS?
Un libro para niños sobre el SIDA

WATERFRONT BOOKS
85 Crescent Road   Burlington, VT 05401
Order toll-free: 1-800-639-6063